JUST A FLING

MAYA JEAN

Alpha read by JJ and Hannah

Beta read by Lexi and Donatella

Edited by L.C. Valentine

Proofread by Judy's Proofreading

Cover by Black Jazz Design

❀ Formatted with Vellum

For Amber,
Courage found us when we needed it most. Thank you isn't strong enough, so I'll give my best story to you instead.

FOREWORD

This short story was initially featured in the *Love in Tuscany* anthology along with stories from J.J. Mulder and Hannah Henry. No additional words have been added and the story has not been changed. If this is your first time reading, enjoy the sweeping romance. If not, thanks for visiting again.

CONTENT AND TRIGGER WARNINGS

- Mentions of past child abuse
- Mentions of past cheating by a spouse
- Foster care system

CHAPTER ONE

TATE

Even a year after my divorce, the pain still stings like a fresh wound. But it especially burns at the idea of a romantic week in Tuscany to celebrate my half sister's wedding. Reconciling my joy for her finding happiness with the bitter pill of watching someone get a fresh start after my marriage crashed and burned, well, it's seemingly impossible. At some point, I've stopped believing in love, assuming that maybe it's meant only for other people but never for me. Evan made sure I stopped believing in love through our bitter, drawn-out divorce.

I am going to stop thinking about my ex-husband.

The affirmation hasn't worked in a year, but if I say it enough, it'll surely come true, especially since he's not worth my time. The asshole cheated on me throughout our entire marriage and then had the gall to blame *me* because I "work all the time." I'm an on-call cardiac surgeon with one of the largest hospitals in Portland, Oregon. Of course, I work all the time.

Anyway, I digress.

Tuscany for a week.

The beautiful hills of the countryside rise and fall outside the car window. Something about the sight eases the tight tension around my permanently cracked heart. I've tried so hard, for so long, to be *enough* for everyone. My parents divorced when I was twelve, my father remarried to Olivia's mom. Now Olivia is the favorite, for which I can't even fault her, because she's perfect—bright sunshine after a long cloudy week, a sip of sweet tea on a hot summer's day. And I'm excited to celebrate her for a week, so I just need to plaster a smile on my face and make do.

I tip the driver, grab my bags, and steel myself as I look up at the grand villa I'll spend the next week in with close family and friends before the larger circle arrives for the wedding day and reception. Olivia's marrying some fancy football player that also thinks the sun shines out of her ass, which it does, so at least he's a good guy.

"Tate!" Olivia screams while running full tilt toward me.

At that moment, she looks so much like the toddler that had chased me everywhere in my teens that I could almost weep with grief over time lost. Time is an awful thief. I squeeze her tightly before tugging her away to gaze down at her. She smiles knowingly, then promptly flicks my nose, making me sigh. It's a game we've played since the dawn of time.

"Is Dad here?"

"Inside," Olivia replies as she grabs my hand tight, turns, and promptly heads up the steep gravel driveway.

The sun is so bright, and the wind blows through the trees as it softly makes its way over the hills. Tuscany is beautiful, exactly what I needed after years tucked away in Portland, away from everyone. The large villa has twenty bedrooms in the main house and a few secluded buildings in the back for the family. No clue where Olivia will be putting me, but after the flight, a nap sure sounds nice. It's like when I turned forty, my body decided that any time could be nap time. Probably a bit of the depression, too.

"How was the flight?" Olivia asks.

I shrug. "Normal. Beat to hell now, though."

"I figured you'd need a nap, what with the time change. If you nap this afternoon, you can join us for dinner. By then, almost everyone should be here."

Laughter rings out through the open doors leading to the backyard. I squint into the midday sun and shield my eyes with my hand to catch a peek at the mingling people down below. I can't make anyone out, but they're all having fun. Good for them.

"Hey, kiddo," Dad calls out from where he's sitting with a glass of wine on the shaded porch. Forty years old, and my dad still calls me kiddo. I can't help but smile.

After a tight hug and some brief catching up about my flight, Olivia saves me by dragging me away from the porch to lead me up to my room. It's one of the nicer rooms on the third floor, and the view of the hills sprawling behind the property is both simultaneously serene and magical. The room is airy and fresh, with cream-colored curtains that softly float in the warm, gentle breeze coming through the window. Yeah, this is just what I needed, even despite the lovefest the next week will hurl at me.

"Thank you for coming," Olivia says softly.

I spin around to stare at her. "Why wouldn't I come?"

"I know it's hard for you to get away…" Olivia trails off as if just realizing what she's said. Despite our age difference, we've always been quite close, and she listened to me sob over the phone for many nights after Evan broke my heart into pieces.

"I will always make time for you. Always."

I kiss her cheek right before she leaves me alone for a nap. After showering the smell of plane off me, I stand in front of the mirror and don't recognize the man staring back at me. Sure, it's the same dark hair, a little gray sprinkled in now, and the same dark brown eyes, but I'm still wholly unremarkable. I've always focused more on my career than life outside of it. I've always done what I thought I *should*, not necessarily what I wanted. I love my job, don't get me wrong. But I don't know who I am outside of it anymore. For years, it was medical school, residency, a fellowship, and then just work, which finally burned my marriage to the ground. What do I want for the rest of my life?

For now, I want to have a nap.

I snuggle into the soft, downy bed, the gentle breeze fanning over me, the warm sun on my face, and fall asleep in moments.

When I rouse from my nap, I wake up in another world. The sky outside is a dark orange, turning purple as my eyes blink away the lingering haze of sleep. Muffled laughter floats in from below, and the smell of food makes my stomach rumble with hunger. God, I haven't eaten in at least a day. Par for the course for me. Rubbing the last bits of sleep from my eyes, I roll out of bed and pad to my suitcase and garment bag that I tossed haphazardly into the corner. After dressing in cream linen pants and a dark blue button-down, I spend a few moments taming my dark, slightly curly hair. It'll have to do, and at least my neatly trimmed beard is still holding up for now.

The same smell of food and the sound of cutlery greets me

as I descend the steps down to the first floor. Olivia hastily exits the kitchen with a chilled glass of wine and a wide grin on her lips just as I'm wondering if I awoke in another dimension.

"I tried to wake you an hour ago, but you were dead to the world. Sorry, I know you'll probably not sleep tonight now."

I snort. "Don't worry, I can sleep some more. Is everyone here?"

She tilts her head toward the porch. "Mostly, just the family, some of Bailey's friends and family. Maybe you'll meet someone this weekend." Olivia wiggles her eyebrows. "Want some wine?"

"God, yes."

We head back into the kitchen momentarily so she can grab me a glass of wine from the varying bottles on the large chef's island. Thankfully, she knows my taste better than anyone and grabs me a dark cabernet. The kitchen staff smile indulgently at us, before shooing us out of the kitchen to enjoy the dinner. Nobody quiets as we exit onto the porch, which works wonders for my nerves. Olivia sits me in the empty seat beside Dad. I lean forward to wave at Olivia's mom, Gloria, before fixing myself a plate of whatever the pasta is that smells like heaven on earth.

"You look tired," Dad comments from the corner of his mouth.

"Just had a six-hour nap. I feel great."

"Work?" Dad prods.

I shrug, not wanting to worry him more than he already worries. I'd moved away from home on the East Coast to the South for college and then ended up on the West Coast for residency. Laziness made me end up staying on the West Coast for good. I rarely see him, my stepmom, or Olivia unless I make the long trek home. It'll be nicer now that Olivia's soon-to-be husband was traded to the NFL team in Seattle with a decent contract. Hopefully, if she has children, they'll get to know Uncle Tate instead of me being some weird mirage that sends them presents on major holidays.

The pasta is heavenly, and the wine is the right amount of bitter. Stars begin to dot the sky as everyone happily chats while they eat the delicious food. For the first time in a long time, I feel relaxed, my shoulders not tense to my ears. Once the main meal and our dishes are cleared away, the staff set plates of rich-looking cake in front of each of us. Two bites in, and I can't eat any more. Pushing the plate away, I let my gaze float over the table. My gaze snags on Olivia and we exchange smiles just as Bailey stands to make some sort of toast.

"Hey, everyone, thanks for coming. I know everyone is suffering from varying degrees of jet lag, but we wanted to get everyone together for a meal before the wedding week adventures kick off." Bailey pauses to look down at Olivia with the softest, most love-sickening look on earth. Ugh. "We just wanted everyone to have a good time this week, relax, and have fun. We want our family and friends to have a vacation. While there aren't any hard-core planned events, there's much to do here! Feel free to team up to do things together or venture off on your own; make of the time what you will." Bailey pauses to chuckle. "As long as you're ready to celebrate with us on Saturday."

Not to be an asshole or anything, but I zone out the rest. Leaning back in my chair, I sip at the wine as everyone continues to chat through their desserts. The sky here is so dark that the stars are the brightest I've ever seen, probably from lack of light pollution. I've always been more of a city guy, so seeing a real night sky has been rare. Once dinner and dessert are over, everyone continues to talk, but the jet lag still weighs me down, so I'm not in the mood for forced socializing. With a kiss on Olivia's cheek and a cool glass of wine tucked in my hand, I head to the garden at the back of the large villa.

A cool breeze washes over me, and I close my eyes to drink in the heady moment.

"Hey," a voice calls from behind me.

Startled, I almost drop my wine but quickly recover easily as I spin to turn around. I blink slowly as I take in the man standing before me. Broad shoulders, a thick waist, tousled golden blond hair, and a clean-shaven face. He looks young, probably Bailey's age.

"Hello," I reply like the idiot that I am.

The man steps forward and holds out his hand with a shy smile. "I'm Sully, or, well, Sullivan. But everyone calls me Sully."

I shake his offered hand, noting his firm grip and the calluses on his fingertips. Our hands hold for a little longer than they need to as my heart speeds up ever so slightly.

"Tate."

Sully grins and nods. "I know, Olivia's older brother."

"Half-brother," I quickly correct him.

Sully tilts his head like a puppy. "Same difference."

Taking a sip of my wine, I hum in indifference. "How do you know Bailey?"

"We played together in high school and college."

Ah, football player. That makes sense. "What do you do now?"

That pulls a chuckle from Sully. He has a nice, deep, warm laugh, and the sound moves through me like the breeze over my skin. "I still play football. I'm just not a big, fancy quarterback like Bailey. I'm a defensive safety."

A blush works its way up my neck as I stare at him. "I know absolutely nothing about football."

Sully shrugs his broad shoulders. "It's just my job. What do you do?"

"I'm a cardiac surgeon."

Sully blinks slowly. "Heart surgeon?"

I lift my wineglass with a smile. "Yep."

"I bet that's stressful."

"You can say that again."

Sully steps closer to me so that I can feel the heat radiating off of him. He smells nice, a little smoky, with a hint of spice. It's a warm smell that oddly settles my nerves.

"So, you're between seasons now, right? I know that much about football."

Sully gives me this puzzled look before taking a sip of his wine. "Yes, we head back to pre-season training in a few weeks. That's why Bailey picked now for the wedding so he can enjoy his time off, enjoy the honeymoon."

I nod as if I understand. "Makes sense."

Sully chuckles, soft and low. "Do you even know when the season is?"

I at least have the decency to give him a sheepish look. "Guilty as charged, I don't. I'm not much of a sports guy."

Sully takes a step further into the garden, and I follow as if tied to him by a string. Our arms brush gently; my shoulder brushes his bicep since he has enough inches on me that I have to look up a little when we speak. A shiver passes over me in the dark as the breeze picks up again, causing Sully's blond hair to ruffle delightfully in the wind. He's beautiful.

"So, what do you do for fun?"

I blink slowly, then frown as I try to think up something. What do I do for fun? Such a horrible little three-letter word.

"I used to rock climb back in college and during residency."

Sully's eyes light up. "I love to rock climb! Well, I used to. I'm over the weight limit for most gyms now, so I can only belay. You don't climb anymore?"

"No," I say sadly, swishing the wine in my glass as we walk. "I don't have much time anymore with work. I still have all of my gear… just never go."

Sully sends a frown my way, then looks back up at the sky as we walk aimlessly. "That's sad. It's fun. Even though most gyms have that auto-belay feature now."

"Mmm, yes. The best part is trusting your partner and them guiding you when you're stuck on a tough route."

Sully all-out grins again. He's got a nice mouth, and his eyes crinkle at the corners when he grins. Oh boy. I feel myself flush and tear my gaze away from him before I can start thinking dangerous thoughts. It's been so long since I felt intimacy, not even just sex, but true intimacy, like holding a lover's hand as we walk down the sidewalk after dinner or someone spooning behind me in the middle of the night when they're cold. I might've been bad at marriage, but I enjoy the intimacy of a partner, of being loved.

"It's lovely here." Sully glances over at me, then back ahead as if caught looking at me. "I got in this morning, napped, then swam. The pool's nice!"

Sully says everything in a rush, almost as if he's nervous. I glance behind me only to find we've wandered further away than I realized. The villa is a bright spot in the darkness, with the sound of the others faded from view. Out here under the stars, Sully and I are almost completely alone.

"What college did you play for?"

"University of Florida."

I gasp and smack his arm, which is a solid rock under my hand. Jesus. "I did my medical degree there."

"When?"

I roll my eyes. "Many years ago. I'm forty."

Sully shrugs as we stop at the end of the trail. I hadn't noticed how much noise we'd been making by walking on the gravel until we came to a stop. It's so silent here. Only the distant sound of the villa and the wind swooshing through the trees. I take a sip of my wine just as I glance up to find Sully staring down at me.

"Forty isn't old," Sully says matter-of-factly.

I blink up at him. "I know."

"I'm thirty." Sully runs a hand through his hair, oddly making him look even more attractive. I've never been someone who has a "type," but I think if I did, it would be someone exactly like Sully. My throat feels thick as I imagine wrapping my arms around his neck, him lifting me up, him tossing me around like a rag doll. Yeah, bad train of thought. Bad Tate.

"Lots of life left to live," I reply because I don't know what else to say.

"I'm probably going to retire soon," Sully says softly, like a secret shared only with me. "I injured my shoulder a couple of seasons ago, and it hurts more and more each year."

As if out of habit, Sully rubs at his shoulder. I have this odd urge to reach up and touch the tender spot, even more so when he scowls at his own touch. But instead, I grip my wineglass tighter and grimace in sympathy when he looks my way.

"What will you do after you retire?"

A flush steals over Sully's face as a shy smile tilts his lips up. Oh. I dig my toes into my dress shoes until it hurts, anything to center myself because I don't think I've felt this level of attraction in a very long time.

"I have a degree in computer science, so I'll probably just get a normal-person job. I never planned to stay in the league for long." Sully blows out a breath as he once again looks up at the sky. "I grew up in the system, so the league was mostly a way to set myself up for success. The league has a great pension too… I wanted to ensure I could provide for my family for a long time."

"Your family?"

"My future family," Sully says softly with a hint of embarrassment.

"That's sweet," I admit without a hint of teasing. That is sweet. He's so young to be thinking of the future.

"Where do you live back in the States?" Sully asks just before finishing his glass of wine. He tips the glass to hold the stem between his forefinger and middle finger. For some reason, I find that way hotter than I should. When I glance back up, he's staring at me in wait.

I clear my throat softly. "Oregon."

"Ah, I'm in Seattle. I play for the team that Bailey will be joining."

"The Seahawks?"

Sully grins, all teeth and a bit of smirk. "So, you do know *some* football?"

I snort. "I'd have to be blind not to know the Seahawks. What do you do in your free time?"

"I love a good nap, but I love to go for a hike. Oregon has a lot of good hiking, doesn't it?"

"It does," I admit slowly, a niggle of shame working its way through me. "I just work so much that I don't get to do it as often as I'd like. All I do is work and sleep."

"Makes life short when all you do is work and sleep. This must be hard for you."

My eyebrows furrow. "What's hard for me?"

Sully sweeps his hand out to gesture at the land around us. "Taking a break? No work for a week. What will you do?"

"I don't know yet." I rub anxiously at my neck as I polish off my cabernet. "I hadn't thought that far ahead."

"I was thinking of going for a wine tour tomorrow. Would you like to join me?"

I stare up at Sully in the hushed darkness. His deep blue eyes are soft as he gazes down at me, mouth slightly tipped up into a shy but tender smile. I could sit around and watch my dear sister fall deeper in love with her future husband, or I could galivant around with Sully. The decision is pretty easy to make.

"I'd love to go with you," I reply before I can talk myself out of it.

Sully's answering grin could illuminate the darkest of nights.

CHAPTER TWO

SULLY

I fiddle nervously with my shirt as I stand in front of the mirror in my room. Jesus. I haven't been this anxious since my first date in high school. This isn't even a real date. Tate had just looked so fucking lonely and so beautiful that I couldn't help but ask him to hang out with me. Just the two of us. Running my hands down my shirt, I focus on my soft belly for a second, then push my thoughts away.

It's just a little before noon when I finally knock on the door to Tate's room. When it swings open, my breath painfully catches in my suddenly too small rib cage. He's stunning. His beard looks more trimmed and groomed than the night before, his dark hair combed over in a messy, swooping wave. A pair of sunglasses sit precariously atop his head, and they move back a bit when he lifts his gaze to me with a gentle grin on his plush lips.

"Hi," Tate says, sounding oddly out of breath.

"Hi," I repeat dumbly. So suave, Sully.

Tate stares at me, then snaps his fingers and spins around. I catch the door with my hand, holding it open to watch him flit around the room. He returns with a small jar in his hand and holds it out to me, a blush stealing its way across his slightly freckled cheeks.

"I have a knee injury from my rock climbing days, and Tiger Balm helps so much. Have you ever tried it on your shoulder? It's worth a shot."

I grip the Tiger Balm tight in my palm, then glance up at Tate with a rock stuck in my throat. "No, I've never tried it. I will tonight. Thank you."

Tate looks at me oddly but seemingly shakes himself before closing his bedroom door. The villa is strangely quiet as we descend the stairs together. We grab some pastries from the kitchen, wrapping them in parchment paper, and then head out to face the day. The sun in Tuscany feels different than anywhere else I've ever been. My skin tingles from the warmth, the humid air, and Tate's dizzying proximity. I tug the keys from one of the vehicles provided to us out of my packet, dangling them in my palm to show Tate with a rueful smile.

"Got us a car."

Tate smirks softly. "I was wondering how you planned to get us there. I thought perhaps we'd walk."

I chuckle as I unlock the car. "I'm not in *that* good of shape. It's a decent drive, an even longer walk."

"You can drive stick?" Tate tosses himself into the passenger seat.

"Of course, I can drive stick. Can't you?"

Tate deflates a little. "No, my father never taught me. I've always wanted to learn, though."

I hum softly as I start the car, slowly backing out of the spot, then point the car in the direction to leave the safety of the villa. Tate rolls the window down to let the warm air rush through the small car. The Tuscany countryside is beautiful, unwinding all those knots that form in my muscles through the season. My body gets beat up more and more each year. I wasn't lying when I told Tate last night that I wanted to retire. I so deeply want to be done. I want to start a family, create a home, and hold someone in my arms as I fall asleep each night. No more grueling practice schedule and games all over the country.

I'm not exactly closeted, but it's easier to be a gay defenseman because fewer eyes are on me. But the league has a long way to go. Playing for Seattle hasn't ever been hard in that area, so I can't complain. It's a thirty-minute drive to the Val del Damo, the home to the winery I picked for our adventure this afternoon.

"How old were you when Olivia came along?"

Tate hums softly as he rests his chin in the palm of his hand, eyes still focused on the countryside passing by outside the window. "Just a pre-teen. I remember holding her in the hospital, this weird, big feeling I couldn't name overtaking me."

"I don't know any of my siblings," I murmur softly.

Tate turns to look at me, but I can't see his eyes through his sunglasses. "You've got siblings?"

I tighten my hands on the wheel and clear my throat. "A few. But that's all the information the government is willing to give me. I've marked down that I'm willing to be contacted, but I haven't been so far."

"That must be so hard."

I smile despite the nagging pain in my chest. "It's alright. I've got Bailey and some other friends. Family is what you make it."

"Now that, we agree on."

The winery is small but still sprawling. A few cars fill the gravel parking lot, otherwise it's just us. When we walk into the stone building, an older woman sits at a wooden desk. She smiles brightly at us as we approach.

"Buongiorno," she greets us. "I'm Cecilia. Would you like a tour today? Or just a wine tasting? You can do a tasting and then explore the grounds."

She has a thick Italian accent, but she's easy to understand. I raise one eyebrow at Tate, who shrugs as if unable to decide for himself. That's fine; I'm happy to take the lead.

"I think a wine tasting and then exploring the grounds ourselves, if that's alright."

I let Tate go first, mostly so I can watch how his hips move as he walks. Sue me. I've always had a thing for older men. Not that Tate is that much older; it's probably the perfect gap for me.

We sit under the shady trees in weathered wooden Adirondack chairs surrounding a stone fire pit. The woman quickly disappears as we settle ourselves in. Tate carefully removes his sunglasses, folding them and tucking them into the pocket of his linen button-down. His eyes sweep the rolling hills, and a small smile tugs at his plush pink lips. When my gaze snaps up to his, I find him already looking back at me with a considering, weighty look to his gaze.

This definitely feels like a first date.

No, it feels like a second date. Last night under the stars, that brief encounter felt like a first date. I don't believe in love at first sight, not even at first attraction, but when I look at Tate, I feel like I already know him. How do I explain that?

Our eyes stay locked, some strange electricity passing through us without even a single word exchanged. Cecilia's return with a flight of wine breaks our gaze and ruins the charged moment. Not her fault, though. She carefully walks us through each different Chianti, then disappears back toward the building behind us with a knowing smile.

Tate clears his throat softly as he wraps his fingers around the glass of wine. I watch, wholly entranced, as he lifts the glass to his mouth to take a small, careful sip of the dark, almost purple wine. The wine stains his lips briefly before his tongue peeks out to sweep it away. My gut tightens as I watch him, my fingers curling into the weathered wood of the chair beneath me. When Tate sips his wine, my heart feels like it will take off into outer space. I wonder if Tate is feeling what I'm feeling. Or am I in this all alone?

Tate drinks half the glass before seemingly remembering we're supposed to share. He holds the glass out to me without a word. Our fingers brush when I take the glass, and a small gasp escapes Tate's lips. He watches me with his mouth parted as I lift the glass to my own mouth, placing my lips over the exact spot where his rested. An indirect kiss. We repeat this process until the flight of wine is gone, leaving Tate's cheeks slightly flushed from the combination of the Tuscan sun and the wine settled in our bellies.

I stand slowly and hold my hand out to him. His palm is warm and solid in mine. Out of the shade from the tree, the heat bleeds deeper into my bones. The atmosphere, the wine, and Tate's company thrill me in a way I've never felt before. As we approach the vines, Tate's grip tightens on mine.

Tucked among the vines now, I spin to look down at him. My breath catches in my chest at the look on his face. Despair, fear, mixed with an odd tinge of want. I've not even known him for twenty-four hours, and I already hate that expression.

"Sully, I can't..."

I squeeze his hand softly as he thinks over his words. I stay quiet, not wanting to rush him to speak. I sweep my thumb over his knuckles every so often, and he only just notices when his gaze pings down to our entwined fingers.

"It's a week in Tuscany," Tate points out, sounding sad.

"How about a little fling?"

Tate's eyes flick between mine. "A fling?"

I nod slowly as I step closer to him. "Just a little fling."

Tate's breathing picks up, his gaze still locked on mine as I brush my fingers against his warm neck. I brush my thumbs over the soft fuzz of his beard as I curl my fingers tighter around the back of his neck. My other hand is still tangled with his, so I lift his hand up to my shoulder, letting go so that his rests over my T-shirt which is slowly dotting with sweat in the warm air.

"What do you say?"

"Bailey and Olivia..."

Oh. "You don't want them to know?"

Tate shakes his head sharply. "It's not that... I can't mess up their wedding. No distractions."

"I get it." I dip down a little closer until I can almost taste the wine on his breath. "No drama. Just a little fling, some fun before we return to real life in the States. Okay?"

Tate thinks about it for a few seconds before lifting up on his tiptoes to press his lips against mine. Oh, it's like a lightning strike to my heart. Folding my other arm around his waist, I tug him closer until our bodies fit snugly against each other. Something about Tate's kiss feels so familiar, like getting into bed after a long day. I lift my hands to cup his cheeks, my fingers finding purchase behind his ears to tug him closer as I devour his mouth. Tate all but goes limp against me. Little moans of pleasure leave him just as he seems to remember himself.

Slowly pulling away from me, he pauses just far enough to blink his dark brown eyes at me. He's not much shorter; I'm just abnormally tall and large. It makes me a good football player but often makes hooking up hard, as not every guy wants to be with someone roughly the size of a giant. Tate's eyes narrow for a fraction of a second before he lifts his hand to brush the tips of his fingers against my forehead, moving my wavy locks out of my eyes.

"That was the kind of kiss they sing about in love songs," Tate admits softly.

"You're a good kisser." I dip down to steal one last lingering kiss. "So, a fling?"

Tate blinks slowly as if acclimating to a new world. "Sure, a fling."

CHAPTER THREE

TATE

I am out of my damn mind. But for the first time, I'm letting myself get swept away by the tide. After our adventure at the winery, we'd driven back to the villa in the late afternoon. Everyone was up and awake, either chilling by the pool or off doing their own thing like Sully and I had been. I couldn't help but sneak glances at Sully as we'd walked back into the villa.

His phantom touch still lingers as I go about my evening routine. At dinner, I'd snuck glances at him throughout our meal only when I was sure no one was looking. He's engaging, but shy, clearly better at taking a back seat in the group than leading it. But the way everyone includes him makes it clear that he's well-loved. And I guess, in a way, if he's close with Bailey, I have to trust that the man is good people.

But a fling at my age must be one of the stupidest things I've ever considered. I don't allow myself to be indulgent much, but this will definitely take the cake. I can't care much about it when I think about kissing Sully again, though.

After a hot shower, brushing my teeth, and dressing in

pajama pants, I'm just about to curl up in bed when there's a soft knock at my door. I push my glasses up my nose as I swing the door open. I'd assumed it would be Olivia or Dad, but no, it's Sully. He's clearly showered as well, his blond hair a messy pile atop his head. But my God, that smile could broker world peace. Just a little shy but a lot cute; it melts all the ice around my heart.

"I just wanted to say goodnight," Sully says softly.

Be still my beating heart. "Goodnight."

Sully gestures inside my room. "Can I come in for a moment?"

I swallow roughly but back away to allow him room to maneuver through the doorway anyway. Closing the door behind him, I lean against the entryway wall as Sully glances around.

"Looks just like mine, but mine faces the front."

"Ah," I reply awkwardly.

"I was wondering if you wanted to see the hot springs tomorrow with me. It might be good for my shoulder. I'd ask Bailey, but tomorrow is an outing they're doing for a hot air balloon, and I'm afraid of heights, so..." Sully trails off with an awkward laugh. He's babbling because he's nervous. My heart softens even more, and I can't help but smile at him.

"I hate heights too. I'll join you."

"Really?"

I bite my lip, warmth spreading through me when his gaze dips to my mouth. "Yes. Seeing you shirtless in a thermal bath isn't a hardship for me."

"Ah, okay." Sully goes to leave, seemingly thinks better of it, and then returns to kiss me softly. It's not like the kiss back at the winery; no, this is a true goodnight kiss. The kind someone gives you after a date that went spectacularly well.

"I'll see you in the morning," Sully whispers against my mouth.

"Yes."

"I'm leaving now," Sully says, but he doesn't move.

"You don't seem to be moving," I point out.

Sully presses his forehead to mine for a brief second before pulling away. He stalks to the bedroom door, glances at me over his shoulder, smiles shyly, then leaves without another word. A goodnight kiss. I lift my hand to my lips, wondering if I press hard enough, could I carry the memory of his mouth on mine with me through the night.

* * *

"WHAT ARE YOU DOING TODAY?" Olivia asks me the second I walk into the kitchen.

"Uhm." I hurriedly grab a pastry, shoving it into my mouth to buy some time. But I'm chewing too slowly, so her eyes turn shrewd as she tries to figure me out.

"Mornin'," Sully greets everyone as he comes up behind me. He reaches over me to grab a banana and a cheese pastry, his arm gently brushing mine. A shiver rolls through me, even as I maintain Olivia's gaze. Her eyes sharpen even more as her sharp gaze flicks between me and Sully.

"Morning!" Bailey says around a mouthful of omelet. Gross.

Thankfully, Olivia is momentarily distracted by wiping an errant egg from her fiancé's chin. Thank God for small blessings. Sully presses against my back for one blissful moment before pulling away to stand beside me at the island. Sneaking a look over at him was stupid but worth it when I find him looking down at me with a soft grin intended only for me. My brain is full of static as Sully makes pleasantries with everyone in the kitchen. By the time he's tugging me by the sleeve out of the house, I've forgotten what we're doing. Right. The hot springs.

I trail behind Sully to take him in, all the big, broad, large, glorious expanse of him. Dressed in board shorts, flip-flops, and a faded T-shirt, he just looks so fucking *sweet* that my heart does that odd little flip in my chest again. A fling? Stupid, destined for heartache. But something tells me that trusting Sully with my heart for even a week will be worth it. Believing in romance again would be worth the slight pain of loss once the week is over.

Sully opens the car door for me and presses a possessive palm to my back to help me inside. Jesus. As we drive, we roll the windows down, letting the warm morning air whip through our hair and over our skin.

"Are you in the wedding at all?" Sully asks.

My brain snags on the way his hands grip the wheel, the tightness of his forearms as he turns down a small gravel road. I only realize I haven't responded when Sully looks at me with a face full of concern. Oops.

"No. Just sitting up front to watch her walk down the aisle."

Sully hums thoughtfully. "This is my first time ever being a groomsman. Well, best man I guess. I already have anxiety about tripping down the aisle or something."

"You're not going to trip down the aisle," I rush to reassure him. But Sully just rolls his eyes with a smirk, a soft dusting of crimson filling the apple of his cheeks. "I swear, Sully. You won't."

"I'm so clumsy in real life. I'm always amazed that I don't just trip over myself on the field on game day."

"Do you trip in practice?"

Sully thinks about it for a moment before shaking his head. "Nope. I guess the football field cures my clumsiness."

"Maybe so," I agree.

We smile at each other just as Sully parks the car at the hot springs. The air is more humid here, probably from all the water, but it's a short walk to the springs. A few people are already in the water, laughter ringing out through the air. Sully tugs me again by the sleeve of my shirt toward a hidden alcove with trees, creating the perfect shade. He drags off his shirt and heads toward the springs without any modesty. I hesitate for a moment, not embarrassed about my body but calculating our vast differences.

Sully's body is strong, built for taking other men down on the field for a living. Mine is soft with age, built for standing for long hours doing surgery. But when Sully climbs into the water like some sort of blond, built-like-a Mack-truck god, every self-conscious thought disappears from my brain when he turns around to aim that aw-shucks smile at me.

The water is the perfect temperature as I step in, slowly approaching Sully. His eyes take me in, full of want and fire, and my body heats just from that single look.

I dip down low enough to be covered up to my shoulders. "This was a fun idea."

Sully steps a little closer, making ripples between us. His hand reaches out to curl his fingers around my wrist, then he gently yanks until we're face to face in the warm water. I can't say how long we stand there, breathing each other in. Seconds, minutes, and hours; time just freezes. His eyelashes are blond, perfectly framing his impossibly beautiful blue eyes. He has a scar between his eyebrows that piques my curiosity. With my free hand, I slowly brush my wet fingertips across the scar, leaving droplets in my wake.

"How'd you get this?" I ask quietly, voice barely a whisper.

"Foster dad threw a beer bottle at me," Sully says lowly, as if embarrassed.

"No," I whisper before brushing my lips over the scar. "No, Sully."

Sully wraps his arms around me and tugs me tight against the hard line of his body. I go easily, not putting up an ounce of fight. Something about Sully bleeds all the fight from my body. Before I change my mind, I wrap my arms around his neck and kiss him right on the mouth. His hands come up to tangle in the hairs at the nape of my neck, tilting my head as he moans against my lips. Opening up for him, his tongue dips into my mouth to taste me, and I'm surprised to realize the loud keen that reaches my ears came from me.

His large palm tenderly caresses the curve of my ass in a way that makes me feel so very wanted, so very adored. Everything about the moment makes me drowsy: the soft slide of lips, the sun beating down on us, the warm water. I'm alive. When I finally pull away from Sully, his eyes are blown wide, and his lips kiss-bitten red. Dancing my fingers over his cheekbones, I can't help but lean forward to place one last, closed-mouth kiss on his gorgeous lips.

"Tate," Sully says softly.

"A little fling," I remind him.

Sully nods in agreement, before releasing a soft breath, an almost sigh. We stand dipped in the water for a while, just taking each other in, until finally pulling away from the dizzying orbit of each other's bodies. We swim for a bit, trading smiles and laughs, and splashing one another under the warm glow of the sun. Finally, I tug Sully back to me to gently massage his shoulder until he's letting out indecent-sounding moans. Not meant for public, those are just for me. Once our fingers are pruned, we climb out of the water to lie down on the towels Sully so thoughtfully packed for us. Lying side by side on the damp towels, our arms brush as we stare up at the cloudy sky.

Sully lifts an arm to point at an oddly shaped cloud. "That looks like a zombie bunny."

I snort. "Why zombie? Also, I see angry koala."

Sully drops his arm back to the ground, reaching over to delicately tangle his fingers with mine. "Definitely a zombie bunny."

I use my other arm to point out another cloud. "That's a ninja turtle."

"No way! Mutant bigfoot."

"What the fuck?" I ask with a stunned chuckle. Turning my head, I find Sully's gaze already on me, with a soft, heartsick-looking smile. *Just a fling,* I remind myself, when the sight of his smile knocks too many emotions loose inside me.

"I like your laugh," Sully says as if the admission costs him a great deal.

"I like your smile."

"Yeah? I keep thinking of getting my gap fixed."

"No way," I say roughly. I love the gap between his two front teeth. It adds to his charm. "Never ever get rid of that."

"Okay," Sully quickly agrees.

"Why don't you like your gap?"

"Got made fun of a lot for it."

"That'll do it."

Sully lifts my hand to tenderly brush his lips over my palm. "Tell me about you?"

"What do you want to know?"

A shiver passes through me when Sully flips my hand over to kiss each knuckle, then the top of my wrist. "Why are you at a wedding alone? You're amazing. You should be treated like a king every day, well-loved."

I close my eyes as the pain lances through me. I've known him two days, and already he sees to the core of me. Evan never even saw me that well after our years of marriage.

"I'm divorced. It didn't end well... he cheated, blamed me for his bad behavior."

Sully's eyes darken. "There's never a reason to cheat, and most definitely no reason to cheat on you."

God. If only he knew. I don't want to talk about it anymore though, so I roll over, uncaring about the rocks between our two towels now digging into my side. Sully's skin is sun-warm beneath my palm as I caress the side of his face. He turns his head into my hand ever so slightly, eyes never leaving mine. I dip down and kiss him again, just a soft brush of mouths, but it says more than any exchange of words could ever say.

"Hey, Sully?" I murmur against Sully's slack lips.

"Mhmm." Sully hums, sounding drowsy, and oh so perfect.

"Does our fling include sex?"

Sully lifts his hand to wrap his palm around the nape of my neck. His eyes widen, lips frozen against mine. We stare at each other for a long time, the sun throwing shadows as the wind whips through the tree branches overhead.

"It could, if you want. But I'm happy just to kiss you, hold you. Sometimes that's enough for me."

"Yeah, me too," I whisper softly. "Sex hasn't ever been a big part of my life, but I think maybe, it would be nice to have sex with you. If you want. To have sex with me that is."

"We'll see where the fling takes us. Okay?"

I nod against his tight hold. "Okay."

Then we make out under the warm Tuscan sun like a bunch of wild teenagers. Sully makes me feel young, makes everything feel limitless and like time is suspended.

* * *

THE SUN HANGS low in the sky when we finally decide to drive back to the villa. A slight sunburn tingles the skin under my eyes and over my shoulders, but Sully's golden skin has only turned a shade darker. Something about Sully just glows. His smile, and the crinkle of his eyes when he laughs, Sully is the physical embodiment of sunshine. I want to bottle him up and take him everywhere I go, pull the stopper out when I'm just a little too cold. I bet he'd let me, too. Sully is the best sort of human.

"Wanna learn to drive stick?" Sully yells over the wind streaming in through the windows.

My heart beats rapidly in my chest. "Really?"

"Yeah!"

Sully pulls over to the side of the country road, and we hurriedly switch, not before Sully places a sweet kiss on my lips that has my heart pounding even harder.

Once seated in the car, I gently rest my hand over the gearshift. Sully grins at me from the passenger seat and puts his calloused hand over mine.

"I'm going to give you a quick and dirty lesson," Sully says seriously, but his eyes glow with mirth.

I smirk back at him. "Just the way I like it."

"The way you drive stick is you've got to feel the car, pay attention to it. The car tells you when to shift at certain speeds. After a bit, it's just like riding a bike. Now press the clutch in, yeah, like that," Sully painstakingly explains as I do what he says. "Now move to first gear, yes, exactly. And go."

The car does not move.

I'm embarrassed for only a second until Sully grins at me. "Nobody gets it on the first try. Let's go again."

Finally, on the fifth attempt, the car moves, and I almost scream with joy when we move slow as molasses down the empty road. Sully guides me into shifting the car up again, and suddenly, I'm driving manual. I'm doing it! It is just like riding a bike. I take us all the way back to the villa, with only the sound of the wind through my hair and the engine's hum to accompany the drive. Sully let me have my moment. Let me cherish it.

After parking, I can't stop myself from leaning over to press my mouth to Sully's. His fingers curl in my shirt, tugging me closer until I'm leaning over the console in a way that'll make my back hurt in the morning. I don't give a single shit, though. The way Sully's lips move under mine all but fries my brain. Not a single thought, but Sully. Just Sully, Sully, Sully.

"After dinner tonight," Sully whispers against my mouth, "let me come to your room."

"Okay." And every single molecule of my body feels like it's been struck by lightning.

* * *

"WHAT'D you get up to today?" Olivia asks after swallowing a large gulp of wine.

"Oh, nothing. Just touristy stuff."

Olivia does not believe me. She eyes me for a moment,

squints one eye, then the other. "Did you hang out with Sully?"

I clear my throat and push back my shoulders. "Maybe."

"He's a good guy, better than douchecanoe."

"Olivia!"

She scoffs and rolls her eyes. "As if you don't call him worse in your head."

I grab the glass of wine from her hands and gulp the rest of it down as she stares at me in mild fear. "I don't. I try not to think about him at all. He's a jerk."

"Use a stronger word than jerk."

"Dick?"

Olivia saws her hand back and forth. "Acceptable."

I laugh into the now-empty glass of wine. The sounds of dinner being cooked in the kitchen waft onto the porch, where Olivia and I sway on a hammock. Down below, some guys are playing a pre-dinner football game. No tackling, to Olivia's happiness and the men's annoyance.

"Sully is a good guy," Olivia says softly.

I turn to look at her, taking in her soft blond waves and the eyes that match mine. Our father's eyes. Turning back to look out at the lawn, I find Sully staring up at us just before the football hits him in the stomach. He leans over with a chuckle, grabs the football, and stands back up with a furious blush. Oh, man. I'm down so bad after just a few days.

Olivia whistles as she leans her head against my shoulder. "My wedding is making matches. Look at that."

"It's just a fling."

"Sully *never* dates, has flings, or looks at *anyone* like that. But keep telling yourself that, big bro." And with that, Olivia stands from the hammock and disappears back inside as if she did not just drop a nuclear bomb right on top of me.

CHAPTER FOUR

SULLY

Dinner was brutal, but only because I so badly wanted to sit beside Tate. I wanted to hold his hand as he laughed at whatever Olivia was telling him. I wanted to rest my palm over his thigh as he ate dessert, a little of the creme brulee getting stuck on his plush top lip. I wanted to lean over and whisper something sweet to him, making that beautiful crimson blush bloom across his cheeks, just over his beard.

But I didn't.

I stayed at my end of the table like a good boy. Our eyes caught across the table a few times, and it felt like *magic* in its truest form. Does this make sense? No, not at all. But I'm starting to worry about the day after the wedding when we all go home. How am I supposed to experience this feeling for the first time and just let it go? Just let Tate go?

The hallway is lit only in moonlight by the time I work up the nerve to sneak over to Tate's room. The door opens the moment my fist makes contact with the wood, and I'm quickly yanked inside before a mouth covers mine. I wrap my arms around Tate's waist and pull him close until he's standing on his tiptoes to reach me. He still tastes like dessert, like creme brulee with a hint of coffee.

Blackness surrounds us as we make our way toward the bed. Only the sound of the night buzzes through the slightly open balcony window of Tate's room. He falls to the bed with an *oof* and I fall after him, bracketing his head with my forearms. Tate grins up at me, sending my tender heart skyrocketing in my chest.

"Hi," Tate whispers.

"Hi," I echo.

Tate gently scratches the hairs at the back of my head. "I missed you."

"Yeah?"

Tate nods before leaning up to take my mouth in a soft, searching kiss. I press him down into the bed. His knees frame my hips as he wraps his legs around my thighs. He's the perfect size to feel slightly small beneath my large frame.

"Can you take your shirt off?" Tate whispers against my mouth.

I shift slightly to yank my shirt off, then stare at him in the dark. "You too."

Tate hesitates momentarily before shrugging and leaning up to take off his shirt. I saw him earlier at the springs, and I still think he's one of the most beautiful things I've ever seen. A slight dusting of hair over his pecs, trailing down to disappear beneath his waistband. Slightly soft stomach, but wiry, and my mouth goes dry just at the idea of our skin touching. I lean back down to kiss him again, licking into his mouth until he's moaning from the pit of his stomach.

I might be bigger, but Tate is strong, and he proves it by pushing me until I'm flat on my back on the bed, and straddles my hips. Tate leans down until I can see his face clearly and feel the ghosting of his breath over my wet lips.

"Can I suck you?"

Oh god. I squeeze my eyes shut briefly, then open them back up to nod at him. "Yeah, but I don't want to come that way. I want to come with your cock against mine. Okay?"

Tate smiles down at me, some odd expression on his face that I don't yet have the intel to understand. "When was the last time you were tested?"

Ah. So we're doing that. "Probably a year or so ago. I haven't been with anyone in… a while."

Tate's eyes narrow, his fingers tenderly brushing against my forehead. "What's a while?"

I swallow roughly. "A few years."

"Oh, Sully," Tate says, voice tender and soft. He swoops down to kiss me softly, plush lips and a few murmured words I don't catch. When he pulls away, I grip his hips tightly so he doesn't leave me yet. "Can I take care of you?"

"I want to take care of you too."

Tate's eyes sparkle in the dark. "You will, after I show you some attention. Can I suck you off for a while? Make you feel good?"

I nod because words have suddenly fled my entire being. Tate kisses me once more, soft and slow, with an edge of desperation behind the glide of his lips. His lips trail fire in their wake as he kisses down my chest, paying close attention to the dips of my ribs and the soft layers of fat on my belly. God. When Tate kisses just below my belly button, I suck in a deep breath, and Tate grins wickedly up at me.

"Let me make you feel good," Tate orders softly as he tugs my pants down.

I toss my forearm over my eyes to blot out the sight of

him. If I look for too long, I might come before he even gets a chance to put his mouth on me. Okay, I can do this. Tangling my fingers in the down blanket beneath me, I wait for him to tug off my boxers, but he doesn't. Tate instead buries his face in my groin, inhaling deeply before mouthing at my cock. Christ. Slowly, I pull my forearm away to glance down at him.

Every molecule of my body catches on fire when Tate gently kisses the tip of my cock through my underwear. His fingers sift through the fine hairs on my thighs, petting me, making me feel more wanted than I ever have in my entire life. This man wants me. He wants *me*. I don't think this is supposed to be as emotional as it is, but I can't seem to stop the tide. I reach out, wiggling my fingers silently and asking Tate to give me his hand. Tate tugs down my underwear, then tangles his fingers with mine.

Tate wastes no time.

The first touch of his lips to my bare cock has me squeezing my eyes shut in sweet ecstasy. God, his mouth is so warm. His free hand pins my hip down as he takes my cock all the way into his mouth.

"Tate, oh God," I gasp out.

Tate squeezes my fingers as if to say *I know, it's okay*. His other hand trails over my thigh, up my chest, touching every patch of skin he can find while his mouth continues to take me apart. When the head of my cock touches the back of his throat, I have to bite my lip to stop from crying out. He swallows around me, and I'm gone.

"No, I'll come!" I whisper furiously.

Tate pulls off with a loud inhale. "No, I want to come together."

I let go of his hand, grab his shoulders, and tug him up.

"Get up here, then. I wanna see you come, wanna make you feel good."

"You are making me feel good," Tate says, voice husky as he rocks his hips against mine. I hurriedly push his pants down until he's naked and pressed against me.

"Lube," I say against his mouth.

Tate chuckles and buries his hand under his pillow for a second, returning with a bottle of lube and a triumphant grin. Tangling my fingers in his hair, I tug him down to kiss him, just needing to taste that damn grin. His smile tastes like heaven on earth. Tate somehow manages to get lube into his hand one-handed and wraps his palm around both of our cocks. Fuck.

I pull away from his mouth to glance between our bodies. "Christ."

Tate presses his forehead to mine. "Be with me. Okay?"

"Yeah," I whisper.

Tate braces himself with one arm beside my head as he fucks into his hand, causing our cocks to slide together. Our breaths mingle together between us as Tate basically fucks me. I feel him everywhere: around me, over me, inside me. My emotions must show on my face because Tate dips down to kiss me, tongue tentatively tangling with mine. The kiss is soft when his hips snap hard to make my eyes roll back into my head.

"Watch me," Tate orders breathlessly.

I blink my eyes open to stare into his blown with desire eyes. The dark surrounding us feels like shelter now, so Tate can't see through to the very core of me. Tate's breaths speed up, his hips snapping harder, and I can feel his cock grow impossibly harder against mine. When his breaths catch, and he comes all over my chest, my orgasm explodes out of me.

Our cum mixes together on my stomach when Tate collapses in an exhausted heap against me.

I curl my arms around him, holding on tight, too fraught with emotion to utter a word. But Tate can still speak; I'll never understand how, though.

"It's never been like that before," Tate admits, sounding drowsy.

I close my eyes tight as I press a gentle kiss to his forehead. No, it's never been like that for me either. We're in uncharted waters. Very dangerous territory. But I don't know how to stop it, and I'm not quite willing to. Whatever happens from here on out, we'll have to suffer bruised hearts if necessary.

"Stay with me," Tate murmurs as he falls sound asleep on my chest. We'll be sticky and gross in the morning, but I don't care. Not one ounce. All that matters is that Tate is asleep in my arms, and for one brief second, it feels like my universe rotates around something with purpose. It takes me a long time to fall asleep, even with Tate sound asleep against me. When I do finally drift off, it's to the whispered thought that I wish time would freeze, caught in a snow globe to relive for eternity.

* * *

"Ugh."

I blink my eyes open to the stark light of sunrise. Tate's wrinkled nose is the first thing I see, and I can't help but chuckle. His eyes lift to mine, and that gorgeous flush fills his cheeks as his gaze flits away from mine. As if he's embarrassed. I can't have that. No, we've come too far for embarrassment.

"Mornin'," I say with the biggest grin I can muster.

"Illegal," Tate says grumpily. He presses a kiss on my chest before disappearing into the bathroom. A second later, the shower starts, and his soft hums filter through the bathroom door. I want to join him, but I feel like he needs some time away from me after a night like we had.

Tate opens the door to aim a disappointed stare my way. "Are you going to join me?"

I almost trip over myself running to the bathroom, which earns me one of Tate's gorgeous chuckles. In some sort of miracle, the shower is big enough for both of us. We take turns soaping up and rinsing off, and as we finish, Tate lifts up on his toes to brush a soft kiss to my cheek. I breathe him in, letting the smell of his shower-warm skin suffuse through me.

"Best sleep I've gotten in years," Tate admits shyly.

I bury my fingers in his hair and kiss him . I don't give a damn about morning breath. We keep the kiss light because we burned the desire out of us last night. Tomorrow is the wedding, which means I'm running out of time with this man. But I'll enjoy today, and the wedding tomorrow, and keep these memories for as long as I can.

After the shower, I sneak back to my room to change for the day. Outside my room, Bailey leans against the wall, an infuriating but knowing smile on his face.

"Hey, dudeeeeee," Bailey sings.

"Shut up," I mumble as I push into my room.

Bailey follows me into the room, radiating the energy of a cat that just got the canary. "Spent the night with Tate?"

"And if I did?"

Bailey knocks me on the shoulder with his fist. "He's been through a lot." Bailey lifts his hands in defense when I stare him down. "So have you! I just think… you know, I think you'd both fit actually."

"It's just for the wedding. A fling," I repeat, although it feels more and more like a lie every single time I say it.

"You don't do flings."

"No, I don't," I admit. I run my hands through my still damp hair and eyeball Bailey. "Have you ever met someone and just felt an instant connection? Everything is just... easy? It's weird, Bailey. It's like I *know* him already. It makes no damn sense. It can't possibly be real, right?"

Bailey tosses himself against my unmade bed, looking the picture of comfort and contentment. Tangling his fingers over his stomach, he peers thoughtfully up at me.

"That's how I felt with Olivia."

My heart beats a dangerous staccato in my chest at just the very thought. Even if it is real, how am I going to convince Tate that it is? How will I make this into something real that lasts beyond the wedding?

"Anyway, today's the day before my wedding. Time to focus on me!"

"Nervous?" I ask as I toss myself on the bed beside him.

The smile that blooms across Bailey's face is sickening with its sweetness. He turns his head to aim his hard stare at me. "Not really. When it's the right person, there's no nerves." He lifts his arm to rest his hand over his heart. "She's in here and I wanna make her mine forever."

"I'm happy that you're happy, buddy."

Bailey slaps my chest as he sits up. "Today and tomorrow will be fun. No moping. Tell Tate you want to treat him right, date him back in the States."

I watch my best friend leave the bedroom, wishing that it was just that easy. Because I have this odd feeling that even if I told Tate what I wanted, he wouldn't believe me. Even if I layered it in sonnets and roses, Tate's natural inclination would be to not believe me, to wonder what the catch to it all was. And maybe that's the part of knowing someone too, even if only in a short period of time.

By the time I wander into the kitchen, Tate is nowhere to be seen. A few more new arrivals are scattered around, but I don't bother introducing myself. I'm too focused on finding Tate. I wrap a pastry up in a napkin, just in case I find him outside. The man needs to eat more. The air is warm, smelling of the jasmine that climbs the villa walls. Golden rays of sun touch every surface of the vista beyond, painting the land in vivid yellows and oranges. It truly is beautiful here. Such a shame we ever have to return home.

The word *home* brings that usual ache back to my chest. I've never really had a real one. Tried to make one for a few years, but the house I bought in Seattle always feels like just a place, not a home. How do people make a home? Is it the place? The person that lives with you inside the walls? Maybe one day I'll figure that whole thing out.

A familiar laugh catches my attention. Butterflies fill my stomach as my gaze instantly locks in on Tate. He stands out in the garden with Olivia, their hands entwined between them as they speak softly. Their father and Tate's stepmother stand to the side with gentle smiles. Family. I can't help but smile as I watch on, seeing the easy joy spreading over their features as they laugh and hug, sharing final moments before Olivia starts her own family.

Tate must feel my gaze on him because his gaze snaps to mine. Suddenly those butterflies in my stomach turn into pterodactyl-sized creatures. I'm so far gone and I can't bring myself to care anymore.

CHAPTER FIVE

TATE

How can I be ecstatically happy for Olivia, but miserable for myself at the same time? These two emotions should not exist at the same time within myself. But I'm doing my best despite it all. Everyone has arrived for the wedding now. Most aren't staying at the villa as that's reserved for family, but Olivia is in full bride mode. She's so beautiful that my heart aches when I catch a glimpse of her. Gone is the little girl that followed me everywhere, the girl that wanted to be just like me when she grew up. Now she's going on to make her own life.

I only hope she makes so many different decisions than me.

The rehearsal is taking place back in the garden, with a dinner afterward under the dusky evening sky. Dressed in my second-best suit, I descend the stairs, only to find Sully waiting anxiously. Shifting from foot to foot, he looks so adorably flustered that I can't help but smile. Everything about Sully is genuine and vulnerable.

"Hi," I say from the second to last step. Our eyes are even

now and his gaze locks on mine so heavily that a shiver dances up my spine.

Sully holds out his hand. “Be my date, tonight?”

I stare down at his hand. “Sully...”

“Just for now,” Sully says, but his smile is pained. “For tomorrow too. Okay?”

I swallow around the sudden lump in my throat. “Okay, Sully.”

Our hands fit together perfectly. Sully tangles his fingers with mine, his thumb rubbing gently across my knuckles. I want to argue with him that this is a bad idea, that he has no idea what he’s asking.

Rows of chairs are lined up just inside the garden on the back of the property. Sully squeezes my hand tightly, kisses the apple of my cheek, then helps me navigate to the seat at the front reserved for family.

“I’ve gotta do my part, but we’ll spend the rest of the evening together. Okay?”

My eyebrows furrow as I stare up at him. “Sully, what’s—”

“Just,” Sully interrupts me with a grimace. “After, okay?”

I nod and watch him disappear back toward the rest of the wedding party. My heart is beating out of my chest as I wait for the rehearsal to commence. So many years ago this was me. Olivia was a teen at my own wedding, excited at the prospect of one day having her own fairy-tale nuptials. I’m so glad she’s found a good man in Bailey. Maybe she’ll be the lucky one of us to get it right the first time, make less mistakes than I did.

At this point, I’m not even sure I know how to make a relationship work. I love my job, love what I do, and I’m not sure a person that can deal with me constantly being away exists. But my god, it sounds like a beautiful dream. Without meaning to, I start to imagine that life with Sully. What would it be like to come home from a long shift to find Sully waiting for me on the couch with a glass of wine and a smile? Could I take time away from my job to watch some of his games, support him when he feels like he's not important enough to be seen?

Music starts as my stepmother begins to walk down the aisle. She sits beside me with a hesitant smile, patting my leg in that familiar way she has since I was a kid. The groomsmen and bridesmaids are next, but my eye is caught on Sully as he comes down the aisle with the maid of honor. His size dwarfs her and I can see the hunch of his shoulders to make himself seem smaller. At least when he's with me, he doesn't have the need to make himself smaller. I hope he doesn't.

When they split apart, my gaze still snags on Sully standing at the front of the makeshift altar. Flowers over the arch sway in the breeze, so does Sully's perpetually messy blond hair. The music swells and I know I'm supposed to turn around but I can't. Sully's eyes pierce through me and my skin feels two sizes too small. I can hear my heart racing in my ears, the blood pulsing to my head as vertigo overtakes me. I should be watching Olivia, not stuck in a magnetic stare-off with Sully. But my god, I can't look away.

A small, gentle smile tugs at his lips as our gazes remain locked. I can't help but return his smile. Sully has that effect on me. Feelings I haven't felt in a long time brew to life inside me, my chest warming as we continue to hold each other's gaze. I blink and there's cheering, the rehearsal suddenly over as Olivia is kissed by her soon-t0-be husband. Everyone leaves toward the villa for dinner, but I'm rooted to my seat by a force I can't explain.

Sully slowly makes his way toward me, all broad shoulders

and smiles. He holds his hand out to me again and I take it without a second thought. When his skin touches mine, it feels right, feels like maybe that's where my hand has always belonged. Sully tugs me toward him until our chests brush, forcing me to look up at him.

"Tate," Sully says softly. His voice sends a shiver down my spine. "Be mine tonight?"

I drop my head against his chest. "You're killing me."

"Killing you with romance?"

I laugh lightly. "Just a little, baby."

Sully pulls away, wraps an arm around my shoulder, and guides me back toward the dinner area. I lean into his side, comforted by his presence. Just a handful of days ago I was dreading this entire affair, afraid that all the emotions inside me would consume me, ruin my ability to feel any sort of joy for my sister. But with Sully at my side, it's all been so much easier. The long table is full of delicious-smelling food. Sully pulls my chair out for me, making a flush work its way up my neck and into my cheeks.

He sits beside me, curving his arm around the back of my chair again.

"Do you think you're going to the next Super Bowl?" someone from across the table asks Sully.

Sully shrugs as he makes me a plate of food. "It would be nice if I get another ring my final year, but it's not up to me. Maybe with Bailey on the roster." Sully grins and sends a wink Bailey's way.

Bailey groans and shakes his head. "So much pressure."

"Big-time QB!" someone else shouts.

Sully looks happy to have the conversation diverted from him so that he can focus loading up his own plate. I lean into his side until he turns his gaze to me.

"I didn't know this was your last *last* year."

Sully chuckles. "I kind of told you earlier. I just want something else, too tired to keep putting my body through all the demands of the game. Want something else now."

"A family?" I whisper, mouth suddenly dry.

Sully's eyes sparkle and he goes back to his plate of food. The food is delicious as usual, but my brain can't focus on it. All I can think about is the solid weight of Sully beside me, the weight of his future that he so badly wants to control, and about all the pressure I put on myself that's never been necessary. A mess of my own making.

The stars come out as the dinner goes on, wine flows, and laughter fills the air. Two glasses of wine have me feeling just a little warm, enough so that I lean my head against Sully's shoulder as he carries on a conversation across the table. His fingers draw dizzying loops against my biceps and my eyes fall closed at the tender touch. Oh, to be touched with loving intent after so many years of no touch at all.

"Tate?" Sully whispers against my ear.

"Hmm?"

"Let's go upstairs."

Sully manhandles me to standing, then tugs me inside without any argument from me. The lighting is dim as we ascend the stairs, navigating away from my room on the second floor, instead taking the three flights up to his room. I've not been in here yet. Something inside me cracks and reforms when Sully's hand shakes as he opens his bedroom door. Placing my hand over his, I finish pushing the door open, tugging him inside by our still joined hands.

"Sully," I whisper softly between us. Moonlight slashes across Sully's face, and I notice for the first time that the wrinkles beside his eyes are deeper than usual. He looks sad, no, not sad, he looks distraught. "Sully," I say again just before wrapping him up in my arms.

His arms curl around me as he tugs me against his body. I let him hold me, knowing that he needs the comfort that my body oddly gives him.

"You feel so right in my arms," Sully admits, tone defeated.

I squeeze my eyes shut at his painful words. Oh. This is no good. I navigate through the dark room, push Sully onto the bed, and go about undressing him. My fingers trail the bare skin that appears as I lift his shirt up. His breath stutters out of him, making me puff up with pride that I could have such an effect on this beautiful man. When I start to unbuckle his pants, his hands come up to grab mine.

"Not tonight," Sully pleads, as if afraid not wanting sex will put a stop to our evening. My sweet man.

I leave one hand on his belt buckle, then use the other to brush the hair from his eyes. "Alright, baby. Alright."

Sully closes his eyes tight as I continue to undress him. I press a soft kiss to his strong thigh, smiling when the muscle bunches beneath my lips. Once he's left in just his boxer briefs, I hurriedly undress myself, and join him in the bed. I wiggle under the covers until he follows, then tug the covers over our heads so we're in a world of our own.

"When I was a little boy, I was convinced aliens were going to abduct me in my sleep."

Sully is frozen for one solid moment, before laughter shakes his entire body. His hand raises to wrap around my neck and he presses his forehead to mine. "Why would you be worried about that of all things?"

"I watched this weird alien movie with my grandma and it just scared me shitless. I didn't sleep but for a few hours for a solid year." I laugh at the memory. "Even now I don't like to watch alien movies. The universe is so big..."

"Why would they want to abduct you of all people?"

I snort and pinch his side, laughing when he wiggles closer. "I'm extremely smart. They'll want to experiment on me and dissect my brain."

"Definitely," Sully quickly agrees. He looks thoughtful for a moment, the creases around his eyes deepening. "I have an irrational fear of rabbits."

"Not irrational. They have sharp teeth."

Sully groans. "You're not supposed to make it *worse*."

I lean forward to kiss him because I need to taste his smile, taste his laugh. Sully's big hand presses against the small of my back, tugging me close enough that I forget where his body ends and mine begins. Rubbing my bare foot along his calf, I tangle my fingers in the soft hair at the nape of his neck. Time feels suspended in Sully's arms. I wonder what would've happened had I found him back in Portland. Would I have even given him a shot? Would I have let myself miss out on this perfect man that somehow sees me for me, wants me for me? I wish distance wasn't such a large divide. It's so easy to imagine a future unfurling before us as we date, discover each other, find out if we're as good of a match as Tuscany has made us feel.

Sully's lips slow, his body growing heavier against me. I kiss him until his eyes stay shut, until I've realized he's fallen asleep in my arms. My sweet Sully. The temperature is too warm under the covers, so I toss them off of us. Sully tugs me closer to him in his sleep, needing me close even in his dreams. I trail my fingers over his slight beard. He looks good with it, and I like the way it feels against my skin as he kisses me. Gives him a little bit of protection against beard burn from kissing me, too.

The damn scar between his eyebrows gnaws at me, bringing some emotion to the surface that I'm not sure I can name. Maybe protectiveness, maybe anger that someone could treat little Sully with anything but tender care. I don't know. I can't explain it. All I know is that Sully is safe in my arms tonight, safe in my bed, and safe in my care.

* * *

SULLY IS STILL ASLEEP when I wake up the next morning. I kiss his cheeks, kiss his closed eyes, kiss his nose, kiss him anywhere I can reach until his eyes are blinking open. A sleepy smile tilts his lips up as he tugs me closer to him. I tuck my head into his neck as we cuddle under the warm light of morning. He smells like sleep and warmth, like everything good that he embodies.

"It's the big day," Sully says, voice still sleep-soft.

"It'll be fun."

"Yeah?"

I nod and kiss the warm skin under my lips. "We'll make it fun."

Sully nods. "I've got to get up. Best man duties call."

"Alright." I kiss the corner of Sully's mouth before hopping out of the bed. "I can't wait to see you in your suit. I know you'll be so handsome. Most handsome man here."

Sully lifts one eyebrow as he sits up halfway, looking like every fantasy I've had since I discovered fantasies as a teenage boy. "More handsome than the groom?"

I snort as I tug on my wrinkled pants. "Double more handsome than Bailey. That's my future brother-in-law."

Sully sighs. "Right. I'll see you at the wedding, then?"

I nod, shoot him a grin, then open up the door to peek into the hallway. It's clear. I sneak down the stairs toward the second floor, only to be caught by my father. He wears a grin and hands me a still steaming mug of coffee.

"Olivia was looking for you early this morning."

"Shit," I swear just before burning my tongue on the coffee.

Dad lays a heavy hand on my shoulder. "She figured you were up to something better and decided to leave you alone. Not an emergency. You doing okay, kid?"

I grimace slightly as I stare at the ground. "Better than I expected. I thought… thought I'd be thinking about my wedding. But I haven't been." I look up the stairs toward Sully's room. "I've had a nice distraction."

"Just a distraction?" Dad asks, his knowing eyes looking right through me.

"He's younger… deserves better. Not someone as jaded as me."

Dad laughs loudly, breaking through my momentary pity party. "You're not jaded, Tate. You've been dealt a shitty hand, fell in love with the wrong person. Happens to the best of us, and it doesn't mean that your second chance isn't just around the corner."

"Yeah?" I ask hopefully, wishing it was true.

"Yeah," Dad agrees before slapping me hard on the back. He disappears down the stairs as I stare blankly into the coffee. Today is about Olivia, about her future, not mine, so I'm going to set it aside and worry about her today. Make it the best day I can.

Somehow my room still smells like Sully. I close my eyes tight and take a deep breath, wishing I could hold on to it when I return back home to my empty townhouse, with sheets that only smell like dryer sheets. I take an extra-long shower, feeling bad for myself, but doing my best to hype myself up. I can do this! I can be the best big brother in the world.

Standing in front of the slightly foggy bathroom mirror, I adjust my silver tie. I don't wear suits that often. The last time I wore one was probably for my own wedding day. But today I'm ten years older, salt and pepper slowly taking over my hair, but I'm still the same me.

I sneak down to the first floor where Olivia's room is bustling with activity. Holding my hand over my eyes, I knock until the door opens, and I hear the soft chuckle of my stepmom.

"Silly boy." Her warm fingers wrap around my wrist and tug me inside. "Olivia! Tate is here."

"Tate!" Olivia screams just as I tug my hand away.

She looks gorgeous in her off-white wedding gown. A tight bodice, with flowing tulle that makes her look like the princess she's always been. I kiss her cheek softly, not wanting to mess up her expertly done makeup.

"You look beautiful," I tell her as tears gather in my eyes.

"Oh my god, not you too!" Olivia slaps my chest with the back of her hand. "Y'all are going to make me cry on my wedding day."

I clear my throat and stand straighter, doing my best to yank the tears back in. "We can't have that. Are you ready? Got your vows all memorized?"

"Yeah, Tate. I'm all set. Are you good?"

Her question puzzles me. "Yeah, Olivia, I'm great. Like always. I love you. I'm going to go see if anyone needs anything outside, help Dad, maybe. Okay?"

Before I can actually start crying and ruin her wedding, I

flee the bride's suite and head outside. The grounds are fluttering with activity as the final touches are put on for the wedding. Guests fill the chairs and are walking around the grounds. So many people are here now, it's easier to get lost in the crowd, which is my favorite thing to do.

A few distant family members stop and talk to me, but I genuinely don't care. I keep looking around hoping to catch a glimpse of Sully. But of course I don't because he's off somewhere with Bailey, doing groomsmen things. One look at him would make my spiraling anxiety dampen just enough to get me through. After shaking hands with some more family, I make my way up to the front to take my seat. I close my eyes and take a deep breath of the warm breeze that blows over me.

When the music starts, I turn around to watch, but my eyes automatically seek out Sully. It's easy to spot him at the back, towering over everyone, even the other football players. He's smiling softly as he speaks with the maid of honor, her arm loosely wrapped around his. Last night I slept with that arm wrapped around me. Sully's eyes catch mine and that's when I feel it, that electricity that connects us to one another in some way I cannot explain. Soul knowing soul. Sully grins that bashful smile of his, before focusing back on the girl on his arm to finish their journey to the altar.

I keep my head turned to wait for Olivia, because I can't let my gaze linger on Sully, or I'll start crying, maybe do something stupid like stand up and declare my love for him. After days. What the hell is wrong with me? Olivia looks gorgeous in her gown, her arm looped around our father's. I brush a tear from my cheek. Weddings always make me fucking cry.

I follow Olivia's journey to the altar, smiling brightly when her gaze seeks out mine, before locking back on Bailey's. The warmth of Sully's gaze slides over me until I can't help but find him behind Bailey.

Sully's gaze is so intense, so needy, that my skin burns where it touches. The weight of his stare threatens to undo me. Just like at the rehearsal, we keep eye contact through the ceremony. I should feel like a shitty big brother, but I can't tear my gaze from Sully. Can't break whatever spell that's over us.

Cheers erupt, and I shake myself to realize I missed the entire ceremony. Olivia and Bailey are still kissing, then Bailey lifts their joined hands. I stand and clap with everyone else so I don't look suspicious. Just like the previous day, the crowd slowly leaves for cocktail hour, and I wait for Sully to find me in the empty rows of chairs.

Sully holds his hand out again, giving me the strangest deja vu of my life. "Be my date?"

"How many dates are we going to have?" I ask softly as I take his hand.

Sully's smile is soft and bright. "As many as you'll give me."

I'm lost. So lost.

CHAPTER SIX

SULLY

I need to convince Tate that I want to keep him. Forever if he'll let me. I don't care about the distance. I don't care about anything beyond seeing if we can turn this into something magical, something worth holding on to beyond this weekend.

I have this urge to claim Tate in front of all of creation, make sure everyone at this wedding knows who he belongs to. I've never felt this way about someone before. Never felt the urge to claim someone, make them mine, have someone think *Tate* when they think of me. It sounds like such a gift to be tied to Tate, to his adventurous spirit, his hurt heart that, when healed, will carry me within the safe confines of its walls. Everything about Tate is beautiful to me. The way he grins toward me when he thinks I'm not looking. The way he cares more for Olivia than for himself at times, so evident in his ability to put himself through hell at this wedding after the fresh wounds caused by his idiot ex-husband.

"What are you thinking about?" Tate asks with a teasing

laugh. His fingers press hard between my eyebrows. My lips twitch with a restrained grin. "You look angry!"

"I was just thinking."

Tate chuckles and jostles his shoulder against my arm. "Well, think about something better. Like tonight! You, me, and that big bed of yours."

I squeeze his hand tighter at the mention of this evening. One more night. I want *every* night for the rest of his life. Jesus. Sweat prickles at the back of my neck as we mingle with the crowd at cocktail hour. Looking down at my watch, I realize I'm almost late to the wedding party photos. A couple of the other wedding party members are leaving, so I take that as my cue to follow.

I kiss Tate's cheek, biting my lip when a warm flush steals over his face. "I'll be right back. Duty calls."

"Ah, actually." Tate holds on tight to my bicep, then shakes himself and follows me toward the back of the property. "I'm supposed to be in some family photos too. I'll join you."

I tuck Tate's hand into the crook of my elbow as I guide us back toward where I can see the photographers starting to take photos. I've never seen Bailey radiate so much happiness before. After a squeeze to Tate's hand, I head toward them. The photographers expertly move around, snapping away as we pose for staged photos, and take some candid ones. I can't help but watch Tate even as I'm having fun with my friends. When my time is over, I pass by him as he heads toward Olivia, and I let my hand skirt across his hip. The hiss he lets out makes me bite my lip to contain my grin.

"You really hit it off with the brother of the bride, huh?" Colton teases where he stands beside me, arms crossed over his broad chest.

My gaze zeroes back in on Tate, because I can't help but

stare at him, even when he's not the center of attention. To me, he is.

"Yeah, I really did. He's special."

"Good for you." Colton bumps his arm against mine. "I can't believe this is going to be your last year with the team. Did you wait just to have one year with Bailey?"

"Nah," I say with a smile. "I think I was waiting for something else to come along."

"Disgustingly sweet." Colton makes a retching noise, but I ignore him. All I can focus on is Tate as he smiles for the photographers and my heart skips approximately ten thousand beats when his grin doubles in size as he catches sight of me.

When the photos are over, I wait patiently for Tate to find his way to me. Until I can't wait one more second. Grabbing Tate by his hand, I tug him deeper into the gardens, trying to find exactly where we were that first night. His laughter rings loudly behind me as I drag us deeper.

"Sully!" Tate says breathlessly.

I swoop down to kiss him once we're alone, needing to taste his laugh. His grin widens against my mouth, his fingers working their way into my hair to tug me closer. He smells like sweat and spice and how can a scent be so comforting after only a few days?

"What's gotten into you?" Tate murmurs against my mouth.

"Be mine. Be mine for real. I don't think this was ever just a fling for me. I… I want you. Do you want me too? Please say you want me too."

Tate blinks up at me in total shock, his fingers still tightly buried in my hair. "Sully?"

"Please be mine."

"I..." Tate pauses and looks down at my chest like the secrets of the universe are buried there. A little furrow appears between his brows before his gaze flicks up to mine. "I don't know if I know how to be someone's. Not well. I work too much, don't prioritize travel, don't always prioritize the relationship."

"Can I ask you something?"

Tate smiles despite the tears gathering in his eyes. "Sure, Sully."

"If we dated, if we put in the effort for this, do you *actually* think I'd get mad at you if you had to cancel a date for work? Would you get mad at me if I was tired from a game and didn't want to go out?"

"No, never," Tate reassures quickly. "I'd probably want to video-chat with you, make sure you're okay. Send you some night cookies via delivery, but I wouldn't get mad."

I shrug my shoulders in answer. "I think that says it all."

Tate's eyes flick between mine, searching for some answer that I pray to god he finds. Seemingly happy with what he sees, Tate leans up to kiss me again. This kiss is softer, a sort of vow. His lips glide over mine, gently, like waves lapping at the shore. When I pull away, I lean my forehead against his to stare down into his eyes.

"I want to make this work. I've got one year left in Seattle, then I can go wherever."

"Well." Tate looks shy for a moment, that beautiful blush stealing its way across his cheeks. "I was thinking of trying to move to Seattle? It's up to Olivia. If she has kids, I want to be close by... I know Bailey is at the whim of the league but I think he wants to end his career at Seattle, go out on a high note."

That's true. Bailey has told me he's not willing to be traded again. Seattle or bust.

"I'm willing to come to Portland. Your career is there. It's not that far of a drive between Portland and Seattle. We could keep my house there so we could visit on the weekends."

Tate's smile turns shy. "Wow, you've put some thought into this."

"Had trouble sleeping the other night and thought a lot of big thoughts."

"I like it… I like that I'm worthy of future plans with you."

"Damn it, Tate. You're worth all my plans."

Before he can argue, I take Tate into my arms to kiss him again. This kiss isn't soft at all. I need to show Tate with my mouth that he's every thought I've had but never dared to put into words. Tate moans into my mouth, letting me tug him closer to my body. But someone clearing their throat has me jumping away.

Tate's cheeks are a deep crimson as he turns to look over his shoulder. God, his cheeks somehow get *redder* when he realizes we've been caught by his father.

"Dad," Tate squeaks.

His father waves. "The reception is going to start soon."

I watch as he disappears back toward the villa. Once he's gone, I take Tate's face between my palms and turn his head back toward me. "Do you get it now?"

"Yeah," Tate replies wistfully.

I tangle our fingers together and drag him back toward the villa. The reception has way more people than I'd expected. The dance floor is packed, wine is flowing, and Tate is pressed tightly to my side all through the reception. I can't pay attention to anything but him. When it's my turn for the best man toast, I almost forget how to speak. So many eyes on me. But my attention focuses on Tate and that makes it a little easier.

"I've known Bailey since we were teens. Back then, I didn't have any family, and Bailey took me in without a second thought. He's always been that kind of guy. He'll give you the shirt off his back without a second thought. He's the one that everyone looks for in a crowded room. The day after his first date with Olivia, he called me and fervently told me *I've met the one.* And you know what? I never once questioned him because I knew if Bailey thought he met the one, he sure did." I keep my eyes on Tate as I speak this next part. "Bailey told me a few days ago that when you meet the one, sometimes you just know. And I know without a doubt that he's right. Sometimes souls just know one another. Olivia and Bailey were made for one another, made to share this life and I wish them nothing but happiness. I'm thankful to call Bailey my best friend, and now thankful to call Olivia my best-friend-in-law, if that's a thing."

Everyone laughs as I give Olivia a light hug, then squeeze the crap out of Bailey. I make my way back toward the table, sitting down beside Tate with a relieved sigh. His hand wraps around my wrist, squeezing tight, rooting me back in reality.

As the night winds down, people leave, but the dance floor has a few couples remaining. I tug Tate to the dance floor with me, needing to share a dance with him.

The band plays a drowsy, romantic song as we sway on the dance floor. I tug Tate closer against me until it feels like he could blend into my body. With his cheek pressed to my chest, we sway, and Tate's fingers stay tangled in my dress shirt. I can feel his heart pounding against my chest, like a runaway train about to jump off the tracks.

"Sully," Tate says shakily, breath leaving him in a rush.

"Tate."

"Please don't break my heart," Tate asks, voice a soft plea. "I can't take another heartbreak."

"No, sweetheart. I won't. You're safe with me."

Tate whimpers softly and pushes himself tighter against me. We sway and sway some more, ignoring the sounds of those around us, just two lonely souls finding something unexpected among the Tuscan hills. Did I think I'd find love when I came to Tuscany for a wedding? No. But I did. Tate's tender heart beats the same fragile tattoo as mine. When I finally pull away to look down at Tate, his eyes are red-rimmed, and his gaze is raw with want.

I brush my thumbs under his eyes. "No more tears."

Tate smiles through the tears. "No more tears. Dance with me some more?"

He doesn't have to ask me twice. I twirl him around the empty dance floor, grinning when he lets out a joyful laugh at my antics. We end up back how we were, tangled together as we sway to a beat of our own making since the band is packing up. I glance over toward the table to find Olivia and Bailey leaning their elbows against the table, pressed together tightly as they watch us with blissful looks on their own faces. Olivia leans back to place her hands over her heart, then tips her head at me in what looks like thanks.

Tate misses the entire interaction, which I'm grateful for because this moment is just for us. I twirl him some more, and as he grows sleepy, I tuck him under my arm and guide him back toward the glowing villa in the distance. We walk slowly together under the night sky, the stars a dappled comfort in the sky.

And that night, I fall asleep with Tate tucked in the circle of my arms. He smells like expensive cologne, wedding cake, and wine, but also a little like me. I've finally found a home to call my own, and it's not a place but a person.

EPILOGUE

TATE

Three years later

My legs ache from being on my feet all day for surgery. Jesus, I'm so tired. I yawn wide as I pull into the garage of my townhome. All the lights are off, so I lean my head against the wheel for a moment. That moment turns into accidentally falling asleep for a couple of minutes, because I come awake to a gentle hand gently shaking me awake.

"Sweetheart, come on."

And then I'm getting manhandled out of the car and carried into the house. I squeak softly, then bury my face in Sully's neck.

"I could've walked," I mumble softly.

"Yes, but this is way more fun."

I won't argue with him there. Our cat, Sasha, meows from the second-floor landing as Sully expertly carries me up the stairs. Shamefully, this isn't the first time this has occurred. Nor will it be the last.

Two years ago, after Sully's final season in Seattle, he promptly, and without prodding, moved his entire life to Portland. My empty and scary house suddenly felt a lot more like home than it had ever felt. Sully filled my life with color after so many years of black and white. It took him a little while, but he finally found a software engineering job with a start-up that he's really excited about. I love seeing Sully excited for something, love listening to him talk, I just really fucking love Sully. I think I have since that first conversation at dusk in Tuscany. He's owned my heart since that very moment.

Instead of carrying me to the bed, Sully marches right to the bathroom. The smell of lavender and vanilla fills the air. I sigh in bliss because that means he used my absolute favorite bath salts. Sully sets me on my feet, undresses me quickly, then guides me into the tub. Instead of joining me, he sits by the edge of the claw-foot tub and tenderly runs his fingers through my hair. I close my eyes in bliss at the feeling. God, I might fall asleep again.

"Don't fall asleep," Sully teases.

"I won't," I mumble, but I might. It will be a close call.

"I wanna ask you something."

"Sure, but no, I don't want another cat. Sasha is enough and I don't think she'd do well with a sibling."

Sully chuckles and scratches at my scalp. "Not what I was going to ask."

I roll my hand in indication for him to go on. "Please go on, then."

"We never talked about marriage," Sully says, apropos of nothing.

Now I'm wide awake. I open my eyes, turn my head, and stare at him. "No, we haven't."

"Well, I was filling some forms out today at the new company, for life insurance, and I put you down as the beneficiary. But then it asked what you are to me and my only option was partner… and I like that word a lot, but I kind of think I'd like husband a lot more. And I don't know if you'll ever be at the right place to go down that road again, but just know that when you're ready, I'll be waiting."

My breath catches in my chest halfway through his speech. My sweet Sully. He doesn't meet my eyes, just continues to scratch at my scalp, then dip his hand into the water to rub at my sore knee.

"Hey, baby, look at me?"

Sully lifts his shy gaze to look at me. "Yeah?"

"I'd marry you today if you want, any day, whenever. I've never been afraid of being yours."

Sully grins, that wide and beautiful smile that still makes my heart do dizzying loops in my chest. He climbs into the tub with me fully clothed, splashing water all over the place, and kisses me breathless.

"Let's go, right now," Sully mumbles against my lips.

I laugh against his mouth. "It's after ten at night, they're closed."

Sully grins, leans back to sit in the tub, and pulls me up to straddle him. "We'll just have to get started on the wedding night. Practice. Tomorrow we'll go to the courthouse."

I laugh as he kisses me again. Three years ago, I wasn't even sure love existed for me anymore. Now I've got this man that loves me with every bit of his soul. And to think it all started with just a little fling.

ACKNOWLEDGMENTS

First and foremost, thank you to JJ and Hannah for building this beautiful world with me in the *Love in Tuscany* anthology summer of 2025. Sharing a world with two of my favorite writers was a dream. The beauty of these two exist because I felt safe to share them alongside your characters.

This story and these two characters will always remind me of the hope I felt once finally divorced. I got a second chance to fly. It's only up from here.

ALSO BY MAYA JEAN

Sweet Southern

(escorts finding love against a southern backdrop)

The Husband Experience

The Former Fake Boyfriend

The Remarkable Lover

The Long Refrain

One for All

(college vigilantes and suspense)

Call It Desire

One More Touch

ABOUT THE AUTHOR

Maya spends most of her time imagining happily ever afters for the characters that live in her head. If she's not plotting how to heal broken hearts for her characters, then she's spending time with her precocious daughter. She loves baking competitions, listening to the same song on repeat for months, and discussing the latest pop culture event in a group chat with her best friends.

www.ingramcontent.com/pod-product-compliance
Lightning Source LLC
LaVergne TN
LVHW091813110826
845146LV00006B/1121

9798990606173